THE SILLY SIDE
of
SHERLOCK HOLMES

A Brand New Adventure
Using A Bunch of Old Pictures

by

⚜ Philip Ardagh ⚜

author of

THE NOT-SO-VERY-NICE GOINGS-ON
AT VICTORIA LODGE

Illustrated with pictures taken from
The Strand Magazine
1891–1927

ff

faber and faber

First published in 2005
by Faber and Faber Limited
3 Queen Square London WC1N 3AU

Typeset by Faber and Faber Limited
Printed in England by Mackay's of Chatham plc, Chatham, Kent

Sherlock Holmes © Sir Arthur Conan Doyle Copyright Holders, 1996, by
kind permission of Jonathan Clowes Ltd., London, on behalf of Andrea
Plunket, the Administrator of the Conan Doyle Copyright Holders

The right of Philip Ardagh to be identified as author of this work has been
asserted in accordance with Section 77 of the Copyright, Designs and
Patents Act 1988

A CIP record for this book
is available from the British Library

ISBN 0-571-22758-9

2 4 6 8 10 9 7 5 3 1

WHAT YOU ARE ABOUT TO READ

*'The greatest man who never lived
and who will never die.'*
ORSON WELLES

I have been a Sherlock Holmes fan since I was a small boy, as was my father before me and his father before him. If there was one of my heroes I could meet — fictitious or otherwise — it would be Holmes. I own a strange variety of different editions of the canon, including some adventures in Pitman Shorthand English.

I've always felt that Holmes's humorous side has been largely ignored (with the possible exception of Jeremy Brett's remarkable portrayal of him for Granada Television). THE SILLY SIDE OF SHERLOCK HOLMES *A Brand New Adventure Using A Bunch Of Old Pictures* does nothing to redress the balance. It's a shameless piece of frivolous fun, using some of the original illustrations from Sherlock Holmes's adventures as they appeared in 'The Strand Magazine'. My intention is laughter. Apart from being cropped or adjusted in size in order to best fit, not one of these pictures has been 'doctored' in anyway.

I respectfully dedicate this book to Sir Arthur Conan Doyle and to the original illustrators, starting with that trailblazer Sidney Paget.

PHILIP ARDAGH

East Sussex

P.S. Holmes fans might enjoy working out which stories these pictures originally illustrated, some being glaringly obvious but others a little harder. Details are given on page 60.

THE SILLY SIDE
of
SHERLOCK HOLMES

A Brand New Adventure
Using A Bunch Of Old Pictures

One morning, Holmes burst from the grandfather clock in the corner, dressed as a duchess.

'From this day forward, Watson,' he informed me, 'I shall be showing more of my silly side.'

He urged me to sit in my usual chair, but I noticed that he'd wired it up to the mains.

'Spoil sport!' he muttered, when I refused to sit.

'Do you think I should wear underarm deodorant, Aunt May?' he whinnied, pressing his armpit up against the nearest family portrait.

Somewhat concerned by this behaviour, I suggested breakfast. Using the power of his enormous brain, however, my friend caused his napkin to levitate above his empty plate.

'Oh, do grow up, old fellow!' I urged.

'If you treat me like a child, I'll behave like one!'
he cried . . .

. . . crawling across the lawn like a baby.

Such silliness caused Holmes's detective skills to begin to wane. 'If you intend to catch criminals with that,' I said of one of his crime-busting 'innovations', 'you'll need to make it somewhat larger.'

But he hadn't completely lost his touch. When staying at the Langham, he knew how to bribe a hotel bellhop with the promise of an outsized Toblerone . . .

. . . then went and spoilt it in the hotel room,
by locking me in with him.

I lay on the nearest table and pretended to be dead.
Holmes quickly changed out of his pyjamas and
sought a second opinion.

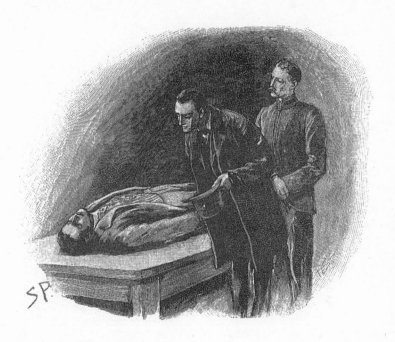

Disguised as a slightly-shorter-than-I-am Indian travelling salesman, I made good my escape, frightening the Grimm sisters in passing.

By the time I reached 221b Baker Street, Holmes was there to greet me.

He insisted that we wear comedy beards during our
meagre supper ...

. . . and then sit through a tortuous game of charades with our neighbours.

Colonel Warburton would have played on all night, if we hadn't persuaded him otherwise ...

. . . and, even then, it took a while for him to take the hint and leave.

Then there was the matter of his equally enthusiastic brother, Ronald.

That night in bed, Holmes kept looking at our
lottery ticket before finally turning the light out . . .

. . . after which, he hogged the duvet.

In the morning, he checked the winning numbers in the paper . . .

When he told me we'd won, I pride myself in the manner in which I managed to conceal my excitement.

Success didn't change us. We still enjoyed the simple things, such as snail racing...

...midnight feasts...

☙ 22 ❧

. . . and 'truth or dare'.

After a while, though, I began to suspect that Holmes might resent having to share the winnings . . .

. . . the clues were subtle, but there for a close friend to see.

My stabbing him with the crowbar had been an act of self-defence, and did little to dampen his nonchalant air.

When I touched him in that special place, and let him use the big sponge (under supervision, of course), we were soon friends again.

One morning, he even tossed a ten pound note upon the breakfast table, urging me to buy myself 'something pretty'.

By now, news of our new-found wealth had spread, and the Grimm sisters began treating me as though I were a 'total babe magnet'.

Holmes wasn't exactly jealous, though he did express a modicum of displeasure when he discovered Miss Elisa Grimm and I boating in Hyde Park.

He then developed such a voracious appetite that I was forced to eat my sandwiches from a safe distance.

He took to constant snacking upon tiny cocktail sausages on toothpicks, made to his own secret recipe.

Eaten in such vast numbers, they caused him
dreadful flatulence.

His hunt for more and more exotic foods once led to our narrowly avoiding injury from an enormous prune in the Pyrenees.

He also began to spend more and more time and
money on miniature fireworks, which he played with
late into the night . . .

. . . lit with giant safety matches of
his own design.

The resulting lack of sleep made him more irritable by day, once causing him to knee Inspector Lestrade in the 'family jewels' over the small matter of a missing postage stamp . . .

. . . and to exert undue force when trying to ascertain from a fellow hiker the quickest way to *The Rambler's Rest*.

He also developed a passion for luring wildfowl to the water's edge and have us beat them with our walking sticks …

... a pastime which he pursued at every available opportunity ...

. . . once resulting in his falling over a waterfall.

Come Halloween, he delighted in dressing up and frightening the local constabulary.

One year, this resulted in a whole two hours of his helping the police with their inquiries.

It was around this time that he developed what can only be described as an unhealthy interest in women's shoes . . .

... which meant that, on more than one occasion,
we were confronted by an angry husband ...

. . . or had to hide from one.

Holmes continued to see clients, however, but was somewhat put out by a Mr James Phillimore who was overly keen for us to inspect his ample package.

Holmes accepted all major credit cards . . .

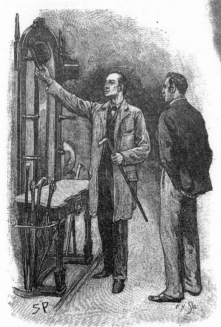

. . . and insisted
that we give the
impression of
greater height (and,
thus, authority) by
hanging our hats on
the highest pegs.

By coincidence, we were, at the time, working for a number of clients of the 'show business' persuasion: Monsieur Dupont, the annoying French mime artist...

... famous for his remarkably unfunny 'waiter with invisible tray' routine...

... 'Doctor Quack' whose singular talent was to play a duck like the bagpipes (though, perhaps, the true talent lay with the duck itself) ...

... the extraordinary Roxbee Brothers, who could only be told apart by their own dear mother ...

.... and for Hans Chippendale 'the Man of a
Thousand Disguises'. His impersonation of a chair
would have been faultless ...

... if only he'd remembered to have first removed
his hat.

After a while, I began to suspect that any chair
might be him.

Holmes's disguises seemed less impressive. He resorted to a single stick-on moustache which he carried in a special case . . .

. . . and a moth-eaten old lion costume which he used for more dubious purposes on more than one occasion.

But, despite these on-going investigations, and his
rekindled love of finger-puppetry . . .

... his erratic behaviour finally became too much for me. His refusal to wear trousers when travelling by train was the last straw.

I'd had enough, so I swiftly packed the bare
essentials and moved out ...

... but Holmes soon
came knocking at the
door of my new
apartment ...

. . . and somehow managed to persuade me to return
to 221b . . .

... where we remain to this day ...

... the very closest of friends.

THE END.

BELOW is a list of the stories in which the illustrations originally appeared in 'The Strand Magazine'. (The numbers refer to page numbers in *The Silly Side of Sherlock Holmes*) Unless otherwise attributed, all illustrations are by Sidney Paget.

The Abbey Grange, 3, 38, 56; *Black Peter*, 13, 25, 35 (top, detail); *The Blue Carbuncle*, 48, 49, 51; *The Boscombe Valley Mystery*, 52; *The Cardboard Box*, 21, 30; *A Case of Identity*, 16; *The Crooked Man*, 11, 19, 36, 47 (bottom); *The Devil's Foot*, Gilbert Holiday, 26, 6; *The Disappearance of Lady Carfax*, Alec Ball, 29; *The Dying Detective*, Walter Paget, 9; *The Engineer's Thumb*, 23; *The Final Problem*, 34, 40, 57 (top); *The 'Gloria Scott'*, 55; *The Gold Pince-Nez*, 2; *His Last Bow*, A. Gilbert, 17; *The Hound of the Baskervilles*, 4, 5, 7, 8, 12, 35 (bottom), 37, 44; *The Illustrious Client*, Howard Elcock, 18; *The Man with the Twisted Lip*, 27; *The Mazarin Stone*, A. Gilbert, 59; *The Missing Three-Quarter*, 45, 46; *The Musgrave Ritual*, 24; *The Naval Treaty*, 32; *The Norwood Builder*, 47 (top); *The Priory School*, 50; *The Problem of Thor Bridge*, A. Gilbert, 39; *The Red*